WHAT IS PAPA
UP TO NOW?

WHAT IS PAPA UP TO NOW?

By Miriam Anne Bourne

Illustrated by Dick Gackenbach

A Break-of-Day Book

Coward, McCann & Geoghegan, Inc.   New York

For Helen and Francie

Text copyright © 1977 by Miriam Anne Bourne
Illustrations copyright © 1977
by Dick Gackenbach

SBN: GB-698-30658-9   TR-698-20413-1

*Library of Congress Cataloging in
Publication Data*

Bourne, Miriam Anne.
   What is Papa up to now?
   (A Break-of-day book)
   SUMMARY: Benjamin Franklin's young daughter
describes the various electrical experiments done by her
father.
   1. Franklin, Benjamin, 1706-1790—Juvenile fiction.
[1. Franklin, Benjamin, 1706-1790—Fiction. 2. Electricity—Experiments—Fiction]   I. Gackenbach, Dick.
II. Title.
PZ7.B6674Wh   [Fic]   76-51272

Printed in the United States of America

CONTENTS

Chapter 1
Electric Fire

Papa is like a child with a new toy.
By rubbing the glass tube
Mr. Collinson sent from England
he can make sparks of electric fire.
Papa makes Cousin Benny's hair
stand on end.
He seems to draw sparks
from Cousin Jamie's ears.

Mama says my pappy,
Ben Franklin, is
always up to something.
I say Papa is the
smartest man in town.
He invented a stove.
He got the streets
of Philadelphia lit.

He is a Pennsylvania assemblyman
and the colonies' postmaster.
He started a hospital,
a school, and a newspaper,

a library,
a fire company,
and a society of learned men.
"Up, Sluggard,
and waste not life;

in the grave
will be sleeping enough,"
says Papa
in *Poor Richard's Almanack.*
My brother Wiil says
our pappy runs him ragged.

Now all his time is taken up
with what Mama calls
the electrical "rattling traps"
in the parlor.
He has little leisure
for anything else . . .
except when he is teasing me.
Our friends and relatives
come in crowds to watch
Papa and Rev. Kennersley
and Mr. Syng, the silversmith,
rub green glass tubes
and globes
to make electricity.

The sparks from their fingers
set oil of oranges
and camphor on fire.
The sparks set aflame
gunpowder
and oil of lemons,
even when poured on thick ice.
There is always excitement
at our house.

But Mama is not amused.
Papa keeps borrowing
her spoons and salt shakers,
her vinegar bottles
and knitting needles.
Once the pump handle
was missing!

Mama found it in the parlor.
It was on a machine Papa made,
which turns a glass roller
against a woolen pad
to make an electric charge.
That is easier than
rubbing your fingers.

Mama found her
knitting needles too.
The tips had been
cut off and
fastened to the roller
to carry off the charge
and store it
in a musket barrel.
(Metal carries electric fire.)

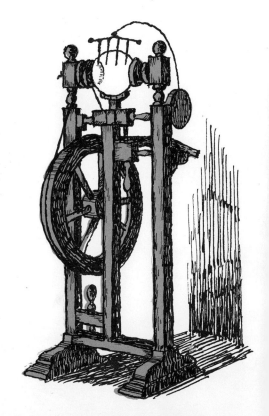

Chapter 2
Sparks and Storage

Papa says Mr. Musschenbroek's
wonderful bottles are better
for storing electricity
than a gun barrel.
Those "Leyden jars"
came all the way
from the Netherlands.
Each is wrapped in tinfoil.
A metal wire runs
through the cork
into the water inside.

I watched Papa
study the Leyden jars.
Then he connected with wire
eleven panes of window-glass
on which were pasted
eleven lead plates.
He calls his invention
a "battery."
It holds more electricity
than a *box* of Leyden jars.
Once Papa used his battery
to charge the double line of gold
on the covers of our best books.

When he touched the gold
with his knuckle
fire was everywhere upon it
like a flash of lightning.
It didn't hurt the books.

Papa made me laugh
with his French story.
A Frenchman fastened 700 monks
together with wire.
While the King was watching,

the Frenchman charged the wire
so the 700 monks
jumped into the air
at once.
I expect the King laughed too.

Benny and Jamie
and my brother Will
beg to be in Papa's experiments.
Once he stood them side by side
and named them A and B and C.
Benny (A) and Jamie (B)
stood on waxed squares.
Will (C) did not.
(Wax does *not* carry electric fire.)
Benny (A) rubbed a glass tube,
giving away some
of his body's electricity
to the tube.
Jamie (B) passed his knuckle near it
and got a spark,
adding some of Benny's (A)
electricity to his body.

Papa called Jamie (B)
"electrised plus."
He called Benny (A)
"electrised minus."

A B C

Will just stood there watching.
Papa told him to *take* a spark
from Jamie who had extra.
He *gave* a spark to Benny,
who had less than normal.
They were small sparks.
When Jamie (B+)
gave Benny (A−) a spark,
it was a whopper
because there was such
a difference between them.

Chapter 3
Points

I beg Papa
to try his experiments on me.
Mama says no.
But today my chance came.
I was sewing in the parlor

when Papa placed a piece
of iron shot
on the mouth of a bottle
on the table.
From the ceiling by a silk thread
he hung a small cork ball
so it rested against the shot.
(Silk does *not* conduct electricity.)
When Papa charged the shot,
the cork ball bounced away!

Papa was called to the door.
I got up to look more closely.
My sewing needle was
in my hand.
"Don't touch," thought I,
and didn't.
But . . . Ouch! I got a spark.

Of course,
I know metal carries
electric fire.
But that pesky sewing needle
was 6-8 inches
away from the shot.

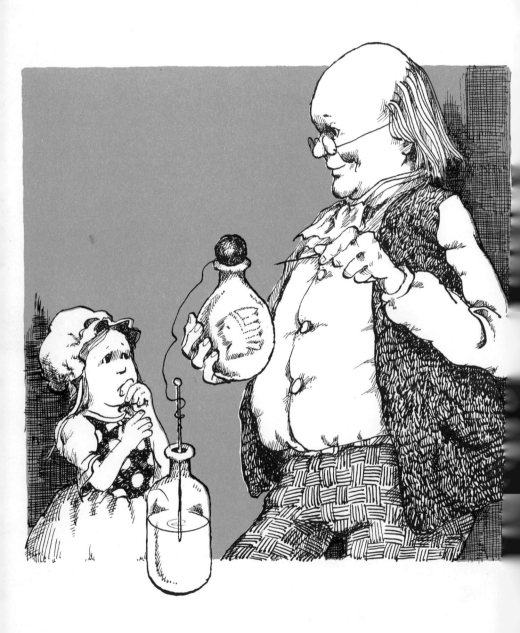

Papa saw what had happened.
He was very excited.
"Did you see that, Sally?"
he said.
"Your needle
carried the fire
without touching the shot."
He took my needle
and tried it himself.
Papa is used to sparks.

"Does it make a difference
if the object is pointed?"
he wondered out loud.
"Get me one
of your mother's spoons."
When Papa moved
the rounded end of the spoon
toward the shot,
nothing happened

until it was one inch away.
Papa got more excited.
"Debbie," he called to Mama.
"Will! Come see.
  Pointed objects
carry off electric fire
better than blunt ones do."
I couldn't see why it mattered.
But I know my pappy.
He'll figure out something!

Chapter 4
Shock

Papa is more respectful
of electric fire.
December 23
Mama went to the parlor
and asked Papa to stop
experimenting long enough
to kill the Christmas turkey.
As usual,
the room was filled with people.

Papa got up at once
and went outside
to the poultry yard.
Soon he was back,
holding the turkey!
"Not in the parlor,"
shrieked Mama.
"He'll be more tender,"
Papa told her,
"if killed
with electric fire."

Papa stood on a wax square.
But as he passed
the electric charge
from the Leyden jars
to our Christmas dinner,
he carelessly touched
the ends of the wires.

There was a great flash
and a crack as loud as a pistol!
The turkey fell dead.
Papa fell to the floor as if struck.
His whole body
began to shake violently.
Mama threw herself down beside him.
I burst into tears.

At last Papa recovered.
The shaking stopped.
My dear pappy's pale face
recovered its usual flush.
"How embarrassing," he said.
But the turkey *was* tender.

Chapter 5
Lightning

Papa believes that lightning
is electric fire.
It gives light of the same color.
It moves swiftly
in a crooked direction.
It is conducted by metals.
It makes a crack or noise
in exploding, and stays
alive in water or ice.

It destroys bodies
it passes through.
It melts metals,
sets objects on fire,
and smells like sulphur.
Phew!
Is it attracted by points?

Papa was up to something.
Mama and I could tell.
He and Will made a kite
from a large silk handkerchief
and two crossed
sticks of light cedar.

Will is twenty-one—too old for a kite.
So is Papa.
He grinned and said nothing
when I asked
if the kite was for me.

Philadelphia was as hot
as an oven.
A summer storm was coming.
I could hear the thunder
and see the lightning.
Will and Papa disappeared.
So did the kite.

After the storm
Papa and Will came back,
as pleased with themselves
as Punch.
"I was right, Sally,"
Papa told me.
"Lightning *is* electric fire."
He showed me the kite.
Fastened on top
was a sharp-pointed wire,
one foot long.
"As pointed as your sewing needle,"
said Papa.

Tied to the end of the twine,
next to the hand,
was a silk ribbon to hold.
Where the silk and twine
were joined a key was fastened.

"We went to a field
with a shed on it,"
Will said.
"Papa took just me
for dread of being laughed at
if his experiment didn't work.
As the thunder-gust came,
I ran across the field

till the kite lifted
from my hands.
Papa stood in the shed
and held the silk ribbon."
(If silk gets wet,
it *will* conduct electricity.)

"As the thunderclouds
passed over the kite,
we watched the pointed wire,"
Papa interrupted.
"It lit up with electric fire . . .
just as your needle
did in the parlor!
When the kite and twine
got wet from the rain,
they conducted
the electricity freely.
It streamed out plentifully
from the key
at the approach
of my knuckles."

Mama was listening.
"Ben," she scolded him.
"If that silk ribbon
had gotten wet,
you would have been killed."
"It didn't," Papa grinned.
"And I wasn't."
He gave the kite to me.
I was pleased as Punch
to have helped Papa.

Chapter 6
Rod

Papa has written
Mr. Collinson in London
about my sewing needle!
He believes that tall,
pointed metal objects
could be fastened
to buildings and ships

to silently
carry away lightning
before it comes
close enough to strike.
Papa has put
such a lightning rod
on our house.
From it a wire passes
through a glass tube
in the roof
down into the parlor.
The end of the wire
is divided
and fastened to two bells.
On a silk thread
above the bells
is a brass ball.

When a storm comes,
and lightning strikes the rod,
electric fire
passes through the wire
and charges the bells.
The ball bounces
from one bell to the other,
ringing them loudly.
Papa comes running,
and fastens wires
from the bells
to his battery
to charge it.

Last night the lightning
was so strong,
electric fire passed
from bell to bell
in a thick white stream
as large as a finger.
It made very large,
quick cracking noises.
The whole staircase
was enlightened
as with sunshine.
Mama was terrified.
She pushed me back
when I peeked out
my bedroom door.

Today Mama
threatened to remove
Papa's new "rattling trap."
Papa laughed and said
he would make it safe.
He is up on a ladder
doing something now.
But then,
Papa is always
doing something.

"Be not like St. George,"
says Poor Richard,
"who is always a-horseback
and never rides on."
What will Papa
ride on to next?

About the Author

Miriam Anne Bourne is a graduate of Wheelock College for teachers of young children.

The author of many children's books, Mrs. Bourne's fascination with history is apparent in her writing. *Bright Lights to See By, Four Ring Three,* and *Second Car in Town* are all Break-of-Day books which take the reader into historical settings. *Nelly Custis' Diary, Nabby Adams' Diary* and *Patsy Jefferson's Diary* record the lives of great men through the vantage point of their daughters.

Mrs. Bourne lives with her husband in Washington, D.C.

About the Artist

Dick Gackenbach grew up in Allentown, Pennsylvania. He studied art at the Jamison Franklin School of Art in New York City.

Dick left both New York City and advertising a few years ago to live in the country and embark on a new career in children's books. He now lives on a mountaintop near Washington Depot, Connecticut, with his two dachshunds. He has written and illustrated *Claude the Dog, Claude and Pepper, Do You Love Me?* and *Hattie Rabbit* among others. The first book he has illustrated for Coward, McCann & Geoghegan is *What's in a Map?* by Sally Cartwright.